Mabel and the Queen of Dreams

Henry, Joshua & Harrison Herz
Illustrated by Lisa Woods

Schiffer Publishing Ltd

4880 Lower Valley Road · Atglen, PA 19310

Library of Congress Control Number: 2016936478

This is a work of fiction. All characters and events portrayed in this book are fictional, and any resemblance to real incidents, people, or Fae, is purely coincidental.

Designed by Brenda McCallum
Cover design by Lisa Woods

Type set in Fontdinerdotcom/Century Gothic

ISBN: 978-0-7643-5137-2
Printed in China

Published by Schiffer Publishing, Ltd.
4880 Lower Valley Road
Atglen, PA 19310
Phone: (610) 593-1777; Fax: (610) 593-2002
E-mail: Info@schifferbooks.com
Web: www.schifferbooks.com

For our complete selection of fine books on this and related subjects, please visit our website at www.schifferbooks.com. You may also write for a free catalog.

Schiffer Publishing's titles are available at special discounts for bulk purchases for sales promotions or premiums. Special editions, including personalized covers, corporate imprints, and excerpts, can be created in large quantities for special needs. For more information, contact the publisher.

We are always looking for people to write books on new and related subjects. If you have an idea for a book, please contact us at proposals@schifferbooks.com.

Other Schiffer Books on Related Subjects:
Trudy the Tree Frog, by Jennifer Keats Curtis, ISBN 978-0-7643-4997-3
Beddy Bye in the Bay, by Priscilla Cummings, ISBN 978-0-7643-3450-4
Evi, My Little Monkey: A Good Night Book for You and Grown-ups Too, by Neithard Horn, ISBN 978-0-7643-3827-4

With gratitude to

William Shakespeare, my parents, and the Author of all things.

Mabel was an expert
at not going to sleep.

"I'm thirsty."

"I'm not tired."

"I have to pee."

"I'm too
tangled to
sleep."

"Will you tell me a story?"
That always worked.

Her mom smiled a knowing smile.

"Yes, but the Queen of the Fae
won't visit until you close your eyes."

Her mom used the extra soft voice
she saved for the best stories.

Mabel sat up on top of the covers.
"Fae?"

"Fae are faeries.
They're wee magical folk."

Mabel's eyes widened.
"What does the Queen look like?"

Looking toward the bed without a word,
her mom tilted her head and waited.

Mabel sighed,
leaned back against
the headboard,
and closed her eyes . . .

Her mom began in the Fae Queen's regal voice.

"I'm no bigger than a snowflake.
Since the first moonrise,

I've glided over
sleeping children,
painting their dreams."

"My chariot is an
empty hazelnut with a roof
of grasshopper wings.

It was crafted
by an old beetle working deep
in an enchanted wood.

Beetles have built coaches
for the Fae as long as anyone
can remember."

"A dragonfly draws my chariot
with spiderweb strands.

An ant in a worn gray coat grips the reins.

When I fly around your hair,
you dream of puffy white clouds sailing
in a bright blue sky."

Mabel's head eased into
the fluffy pillow.

"If I drive along your knees,
you dream of jumping and dancing
on soft, dewy grass."

Mabel slid her legs under
the warm covers.

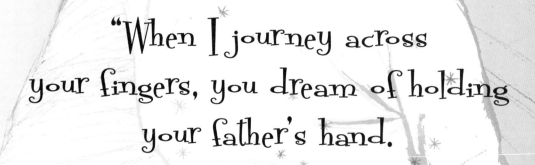

"When I journey across
your fingers, you dream of holding
your father's hand.

If I glide over your lips,
you dream of talking with someone
you love."

Mabel smiled.

"When I hover over your nose,
the sweet smell of fresh—baked cookies beckons."

"If I travel up your neck, you feel the
warm glow of the mid-day sun."

Mabel pulled up the covers.

"Why have I never seen you?"
whispered Mabel.

"I only visit when you sleep.
And I always leave before you rise."

Mabel's eyes stayed closed.
She wondered
what dreams may come.

Author's Note

"What dreams may come"
is from *Hamlet* act 3, scene 1.

To sleep: perchance to dream:
        ay, there's the rub;
For in that sleep of death what
        dreams may come
When we have shuffled off this
        mortal coil,
        Must give us pause . . .

Mercutio speaks of the fairy
        Queen Mab
and her little chariot in
        Romeo & Juliet
        act 1, scene 4:

O, then I see Queen Mab hath been with you.
She is the fairies' midwife, and she comes
In shape no bigger than an agate stone
On the forefinger of an alderman,
Drawn with a team of little atomies
Over men's noses as they lie asleep;
Her wagon spokes made of long spinners' legs,
The cover, of the wings of grasshoppers;
Her traces, of the smallest spider web;
Her collars, of the moonshine's wat'ry beams;
Her whip, of cricket's bone; the lash, of film;
Her wagoner, a small grey-coated gnat,
Not half so big as a round little worm
Pricked from the lazy finger of a maid;
Her chariot is an empty hazelnut,
Made by the joiner squirrel or old grub,
Time out o' mind the fairies' coachmakers.
And in this state she gallops night by night
Through lovers' brains, and then they dream of love;
O'er courtiers' knees, that dream on curtsies straight;
O'er lawyers' fingers, who straight dream on fees;
O'er ladies' lips, who straight on kisses dream,
Which oft the angry Mab with blisters plagues,
Because their breaths with sweetmeats tainted are.
Sometimes she gallops o'er a courtier's nose,
And then dreams he of smelling out a suit;
And sometimes comes she with a tithe-pig's tail
Tickling a parson's nose as 'a lies asleep,
Then dreams he of another benefice.
Sometimes she driveth o'er a soldier's neck,
And then dreams he of cutting foreign throats,
Of breaches, ambuscadoes, Spanish blades,
Of healths five fathom deep; and then anon
Drums in his ear, at which he starts and wakes,
And being thus frighted, swears a prayer or two
And sleeps again.